Loving Comfort

A Toddler Weaning Story

For Jennifer and Jackson,
and my own sweet toddler nurslings

Loving Comfort

A Toddler Weaning Story

WRITTEN BY Julie Dillemuth

ILLUSTRATED BY Vicky Pratt

From the time he was a teeny-tiny newborn baby, Jack drank Mama's milk. He nursed morning, noon, and night. And mid-morning, late afternoon, early evening, bedtime, and all through the wee hours.

Milk was as warm as Mama's arms holding him close.

It tasted sweet like the sound of Mama's voice humming him to sleep.

Milk was like the *thump-thump-thump* of Mama's heart, a sound Jack knew from before he was even born.

And milk smelled like Mama. The most wonderful smell in the world.

As soon as Jack could sit up, he noticed food. Red strawberries, orange carrots, yellow bananas and green avocados. Blueberries, blackberries, and purple grapes. Oatmeal, pasta, spaghetti sauce, cheese. Jack loved food.

But he also loved his Mama's milk.

He loved it in the summer,

and the fall,

through the winter,

and in the spring.

As Jack got older and could feed himself, he didn't need so much of Mama's milk. Sometimes he even forgot to ask for it. But then he remembered. And it was always there.

Until one night when it wasn't. Mama said, "No milk until morning."

His Mama's warm arms held him close. Mama's sweet voice hummed him to sleep. Jack breathed deeply, smelling Mama's scent. He fell asleep again to the *thump-thump-thump* of Mama's heart and the pat-pat-pat of her hand on his back.

That night and the next few nights, Jack woke up wanting milk.

Then Jack got used
to no milk at night. He
slept right on through
until morning.

And so did Mama and Papa.

Then there came a day when the milk wasn't there, at least not right away. Mama said, "No milk now, please wait until later."
She said that during story-time,

and grocery
shopping,

and playtime.
 Jack wanted milk NOW.
It was hard to wait until later.

But Mama's warm arms held him close. Jack could smell her Mama scent. Mama gazed into his eyes and made silly faces and noises until he giggled. They had a snack together and read a book.

Mama talked with Jack lots of times about how weaning happens—that he was nursing less and less often, and soon he wouldn't drink Mama's milk at all. He was no longer a baby. He was a toddler, and growing bigger and stronger every day. Sometimes this was okay with Jack. Sometimes, it was not.

Jack only nursed a couple of times a day now, just before nap time and just before bed. Or sometimes when he was sick or his head hurt from teething. Mama's milk warmed his tummy and soothed his head.

And then one day Jack didn't ask for Mama's milk at all. He asked for extra cuddles instead. And giggles. And for special time with Mama.

It was just one day, but the
next week it happened again.

The days with no
milk turned into weeks.
And then months.

Jack was too busy to
nurse during the day,
and he didn't need milk
before falling asleep.

Now, Jack is all done drinking Mama's milk.

But he still snuggles in Mama's warm arms, which hold him close.

He hears her sweet voice humming him to sleep.

He feels the *thump-thump-thump* of her heart.

Jack still loves the beautiful scent of Mama's skin. His Mama. The most wonderful Mama in the world.

Note for Parents

By Jessica Barton, MA,
International Board Certified Lactation Consultant (IBCLC)

Loving Comfort is about the life of a nursing relationship for a mother and her child. When Jack is a baby he breastfeeds around the clock for nourishment, closeness and comfort. As he grows he begins to experience the sights, sounds and colors of the world, including new foods! He continues to breastfeed for nourishment, cuddles and comfort. One day Jack's mother begins to put boundaries on breastfeeding but she encourages him to come to her for comfort and closeness as always. Gradually, Jack begins to nurse less and less frequently and eventually he forgets to nurse at all. But he knows that he can still count on the warmth, comfort and closeness of his mother's arms.

This story is as much for mothers as it is for children who are learning about weaning. As babies grow into toddlers and older children, they naturally need boundaries and eventually outgrow the breastfeeding relationship. This can leave many mothers nostalgic for the days they were able to provide for all of their child's needs in their arms and at the breast.

Weaning experiences are as unique and individual as mothers and babies themselves. Some weaning journeys may resemble this story while others may be completely different. Mothers who are weaning may be surprised to find themselves mourning the loss of the breastfeeding relationship, brushing away tears and wondering how that little baby got so big so fast. Perhaps it is these mothers, finding weaning harder than they ever expected, who need this book the most: To remind us that even when the breastfeeding relationship has ended, our children still need us to hold them close and give them our hearts.

Made in the USA
Coppell, TX
26 September 2022

83629934R00021